ESMÉ SHAPIRO

OOKO

TUNDRA BOOKS

I am Ooko.

I am a fox.

I live here,
under this log.

I have a stick.

I have a leaf.

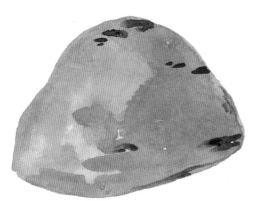

I have a rock.

But I do not have a friend to play with.

Can I find a friend in this hole?

No.

On top of this tree?

No.

Under this moose?

Not here either.

Aha! There's someone! Another fox!
Playing with a furless, two-legged fox.

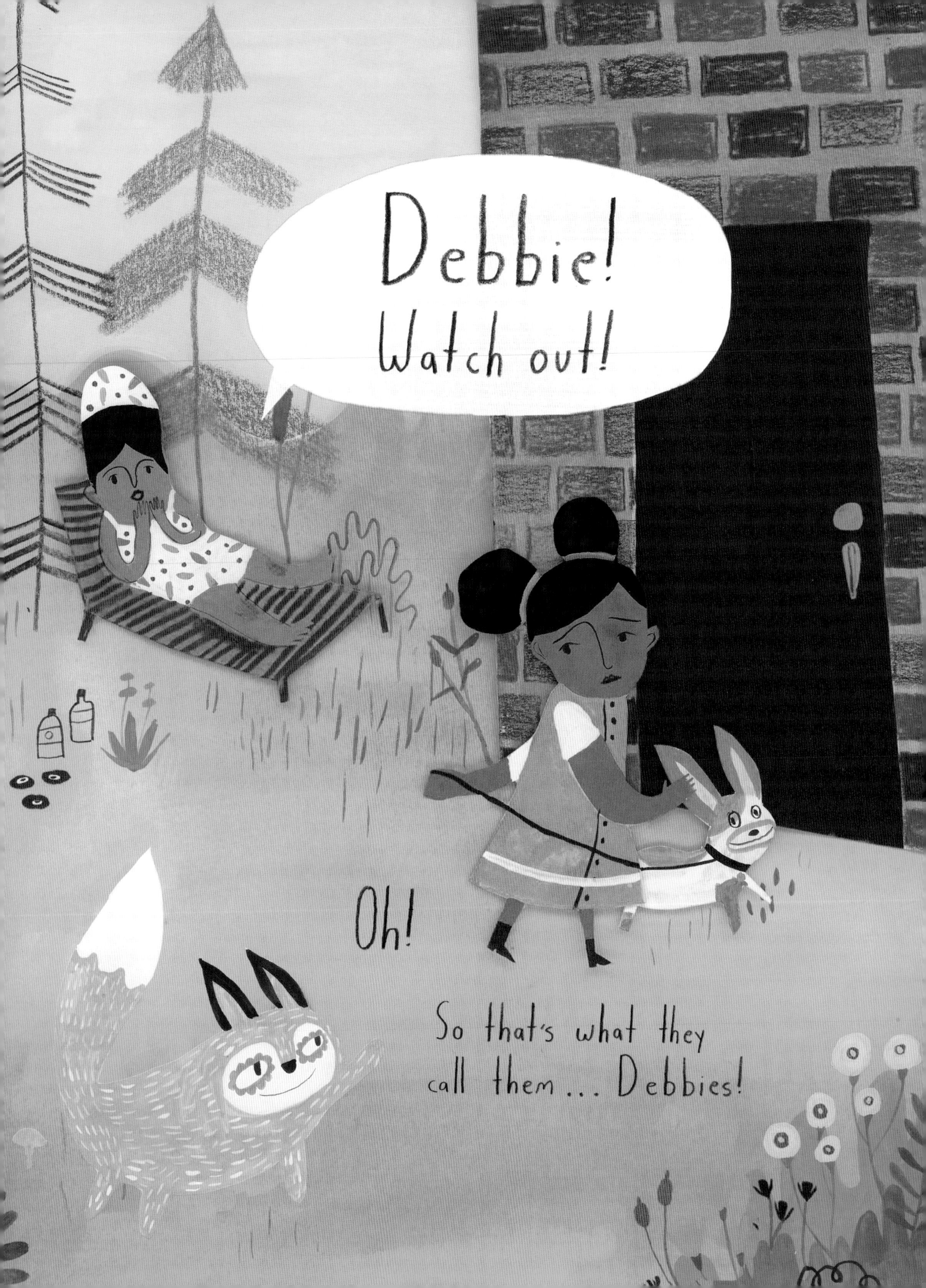

Oh!

So that's what they call them . . . Debbies!

I want a Debbie too!

What do the other foxes
have that I don't?

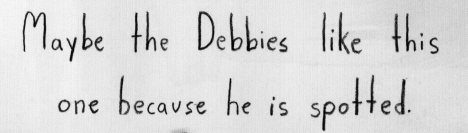

Maybe the Debbies like this
one because he is spotted.

I bet the Debbies like this fox because her fur is pink and fluffy.

I'm sure the Debbies like this fox because of his big, floppy ears.

Voilà!
I can have
big ears too!

Hey, I look pretty good.

YOO-HOO! RUTHIE! IS THAT YOU? I CAN'T SEE! MY GLASSES AREN'T WORKING!
Nope... I'm not Ruth—

ACTUALLY... YES!
YES! I AM RUTHIE!

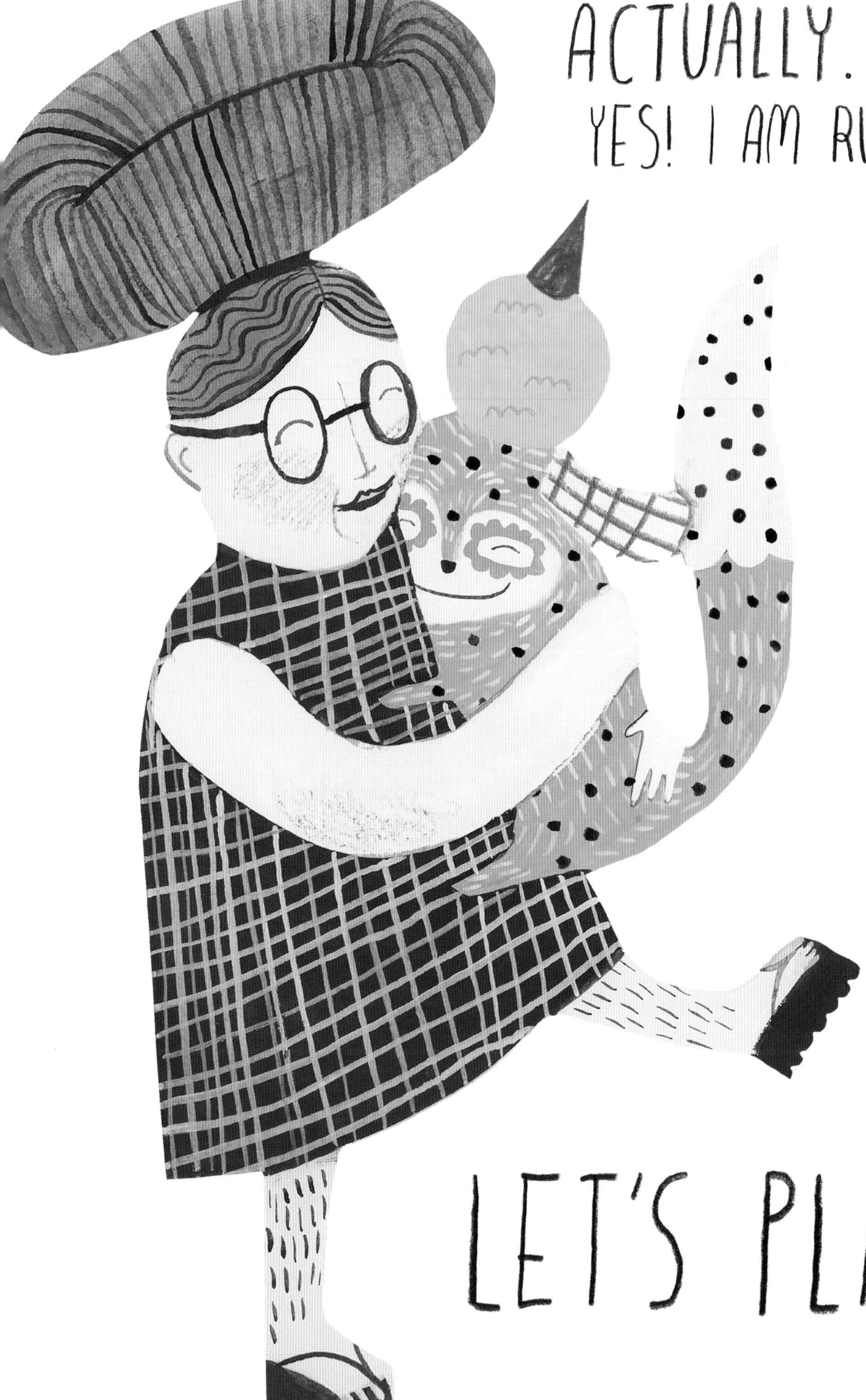

LET'S PLAY!

But maybe not this game.
BRRR!

This game is too itchy!

GRRR!

I hate to say it ...

but Debbies aren't very good at games.

This is my stick.

This is my other stick.

And this is
my other other stick.

WANNA PLAY?

I don't need to look
like the other foxes
to find a friend!

I would much rather be stinky and play stick

than be squeaky clean and play itchy games.

But hey, to each their own, right?

To each their own.

To my favorite Debbies, Mom, Dad, Hanna and Papa
With an extra special thank you to Tara and Charlotte

Tundra Books, a division of Random House of Canada Limited, a Penguin Random House Company

Library and Archives Canada Cataloguing in Publication

Shapiro, Esmé, 1992–, author
Ooko / Esmé Shapiro.

Issued in print and electronic formats.
ISBN 978-1-101-91844-9 (bound).–ISBN 978-1-101-91845-6 (epub)

1. Foxes–Juvenile fiction. I. Title.

PS8637.H364O05 2016   jC813'.6   C2015-905431-1
                   C2015-905432-X

Published simultaneously in the United States of America by Tundra Books of Northern New York,
a division of Random House of Canada Limited, a Penguin Random House Company

Library of Congress Control Number: 2015947648

Edited by Tara Walker
Designed by Esmé Shapiro and Jennifer Lum
The artwork in this book was rendered by a Debbie in gouache, watercolor and colored pencil.
The hand lettering was rendered by the same Debbie.

Printed and bound in China

www.penguinrandomhouse.ca

2   3   4   5   6   20   19   18   17   16

TUNDRA BOOKS | Penguin Random House